The
BLUE FAIRY
and the
THREE PRINCESSES

A CLASSIC FAIRY TALE FOR ALL AGES

A wicked witch places a curse over the land and the three princesses have to look for the blue fairy, who is the only person who can lift the evil spell. Aided by the friendly dragon rider, a wizard, and an elf king, they have to first find each of the blue fairy's three sisters, and then battle the smelly goblins, before they can rescue her from the clutches of the ugly trolls.

The question is, will they find her in time?

This is a story that must be told,
during long winter nights when the wind blows cold.
Of fairies and elves and knights so bold,
who live in this place that is ever so old.

There are wizards and dragons who guard the land,
from the witches and goblins that would turn it to sand.
The villages and castles are surrounded by towers,
which sit in the meadows all covered in flowers.

It is ruled by a king, who is wise and true,
with the help of a Queen, who will look after you.
They have three princesses that are beautiful and kind,
each with bright curls that hang down behind.

Angeli is the oldest and full of grace,
with dancing feet that can win any race.
Inquisitive eyes that sparkle and shine,
always attentive and never to pine.

Indigo is next, with a smile and laughter,
and energy that lasts far into the hereafter.
Bright and nimble, always so spry,
She can jump as high as the sky.

Phoenix is the youngest and fairest of all,
a true champion of life, who comes if you call.
Firm at heart, she will stand by your side
until the others are safe inside.

They play in the hills without a care,
dancing and singing as if at the fair.
The birds in the trees join in with the tunes,
the deer and the rabbits peek out of the dunes.

Sunlight and warmth greet the day,
so that the butterflies and bees come out to play.
It is peaceful and tranquil without any alarm,
there is no concept of danger or possible harm.

Chuckling voices so coarse and loud,
cry out from the sky, attracting a crowd.
All eyes rise up with mouths open wide,
it is too late to run, with nowhere to hide.

Witches on broomsticks flash on by,
leaving black trails in the darkening sky.
Thunder and lightning crash all around,
frightening everyone with incredible sound.

The three little princesses huddle together,
just as you would, in sudden bad weather.
They see their friends tremble and quiver,
and become very cross to see them shiver.

Brave and defiant they look in the air,
for the bad witches, who are no longer there.
Pointing their fingers and shouting out loudly,
the three sisters stand together so proudly.

The air becomes clear, and there is no more hassle,
the princesses jump up to return to the castle.
As fast as they can, they run to the tall tower,
arms swinging wildly and legs bursting with power.

They crash through the gates and run up the stairs,
shoulders together with feet pounding in pairs.
Shouting out loudly to attract attention,
the guards become alert and full of tension.

The king, on his throne, looks up with a start
as the three princesses burst in, not an inch apart.
Without a pause, they tell their tale,
now a little nervous and becoming very pale.

King Mark listens and asks when needed,
the details are important and must be heeded.
The tale is told, and the princesses relax,
Queen Olivia arrives to help consider the facts.

After a deep think, king Mark looks up,
and with a smile on his face, takes a sip from his cup.
In a big strong voice, he announces to all,
that the three princesses are in need of a ball.

After careful discussion, the date is set in advance,
so that everyone invited can prepare for the dance.
King Mark gives instructions for all to obey,
in order to make it a wonderful day.

With so much to do and all going dizzy,
Queen Olivia steps in and sets them all busy.
Everyone is allotted a task to achieve,
including the princesses who now take their leave.

The invitations are sent out all over the land,
each one is addressed and delivered by hand.
Every friend is included, and nobody is missed,
it suddenly becomes a very long list.

Queen Olivia sets out without any rest,
to ensure they are all dressed in their absolute best.
The kitchens are alive with cooks going balmy,
but they manage to prepare enough for an army.

King Mark takes control of decorating the rooms,
his teams of young helpers with brushes and brooms.
All are busy with paint, bunting and flowers,
no corner is left out, not even the towers.

Replies to invites fly back with vigour,
and the number coming gets even bigger.
The musicians' practice to create the best sound,
the noise is so great that it shakes the ground.

At last, the day comes, and all is ready,
people start arriving, and the princesses stand steady.
Each person is welcomed with smiles and laughter,
until the great hall is packed to its rafter.

The princesses start the dancing in a hurry,
each picking a partner in such a great flurry.
Whirling and twirling, they go faster and faster,
it's really a wonder that there is not a disaster.

Pausing only to take some refreshment,
the young princesses cannot hide their excitement.
The rest of the people are now on their feet,
all joining in the dancing, but feeling the heat.

Sir Michael, the king's father, arrives on his horse,
along with the king's mother, the Lady Helen, of course.
The queen's mother, Lady Roswita, arrives the same day,
travelling by boat from a land far away.

Late arrivals keep coming to swell the crowds,
the dancing and singing spill out under the clouds.
The sun moves slowly high in the sky,
and minute by minute, the day goes on by.

Eating and dancing with more and more vigour,
they are all surprised by a dark cloaked figure.
Arriving by stealth and unseen to the last,
the mysterious figure leaps out with a blast.

Thunder and lightning shake the crowd,
a dark figure is revealed and shouts out loud.
"I am the black witch, who you did not call,
to join you in this wonderful hall."

"In order to repay you for this great insult,
an evil spell will be the result."
With a wave of her wand, a black cloud arrives,
casting darkness out from high in the skies.

The rain begins to fall down in great droplets,
so much water that it overflows the goblets.
"The rain will stay forever", she screeches to all,
confident that her spell will ruin the ball.

In a puff of black smoke, she disappears from sight,
leaving them all with a terrible fright.
With cries of alarm, they all look to the king,
who stands up straight and rubs his magic ring.

"This curse is made with bad intent,
but I know a person who can help make it relent.
My sister, princess Belinda, who is not in the hall,
is far away at present but will come when I call."

"As a rider of the dragon, she has been trained well
and will be able to help us get rid of this spell.
With her friend prince Ryan, who rides just as fast,
they are a formidable team that nobody can get past."

With a rush of the wind, two dragons appear,
making the people bow down with fear.
A calm voice cries from the back of the beast,
as princess Belinda and prince Ryan arrive at the feast.

They all rise up and give a good cheer,
now that the brave dragon princess is here.
While King Mark gathers them all for a council of war,
the little princesses run off to guard the door.

With heads all locked tightly together,
they discuss how they can stop the very bad weather.
They need a solution to lift the witch's curse
before it becomes something much worse.

Queen Olivia announces that she may hold a clue,
in an ancient document understood by few.
She pulls out a paper from a dusty holder
and begins to read it to all, who feel much bolder.

The diamond fairy is the queen of the pack
you better be nice, or she will get you right back.
It is only through her that the others may be found
so, you must be prepared to cover some ground.
Over the sea and mountains that have now grown,
is where you will find her on her glass throne.

The ruby fairy is first on her list.
She will grant you your wishes if you can see in the mist.
Magic spells and dark potions are her strengths,
but you will have to reach up and go to great lengths.

The emerald fairy is next to be found,
she is easy to see if you look around.
Shields and swords will be your protection,
but only for those who go in the right direction.

The blue fairy is the final link in the chain
and will be your solution to stop all the rain.
Only by lifting her out of the well,
will you be able to break the witch's evil spell.

Everyone agrees the blue fairy must be found,
but nobody knows how, so they stare at the ground.
The little princesses speak from the rear,
in very loud voices so all can hear.

"We know of a place that was told in a story,
where the queen of the fairies sits in all of her glory.
It is in a land that is far, far away,
just as you told us in the rhyme today."

The king looks up and raises his hand,
and asks. "Who will go and search for this land?"
Princess Belinda says without fear,
"It is clear that this is the reason we are here."

"Using our dragons we can speed through the air,
and find the diamond fairy with her long golden hair.
But how will we know which is the right direction?
It is only the princesses who have the connection."

"They must go with you," they all agree,
and the princesses all look up with faces of glee.
Queen Olivia says that they are too young,
but finally relents when she hears what must be done.

More dragons are needed to carry them all,
so prince Ryan looks up and makes a loud call.
All of a sudden, three more dragons appear,
each of them saddled with suitable gear.

In no time at all, they are mounted and ready,
each person is seated, secure and steady.
They rise in a flash, through the rain they fly,
until nothing is left, not even their cry.

Over the ocean, they see their reflection,
with the little princesses giving direction.
Smiling faces appear from the waves below,
and the little mermaids wave as they go.

The day turns to night, and the sea turns to sand,
as they all look down for somewhere to land.
The camp is made, and dinner is ready,
they retire to sleep, and the watch stands steady.

Morning arrives, and they all awaken,
ready to eat breakfast with lots of bacon.
The dragons are eager to get underway,
as they all get ready to start a new day.

Up and away, they fly straight and level
towards the mountains, which are dark and several.
As they approach from way up high,
something on the ground catches their eye.

It twinkles and sparkles, bursting with light,
they circle around and keep it in sight.
With a nod of the head and a wave of her hand,
princess Belinda gives the signal to land.

The dragons all gather in a group on the ground,
while the squadron of flyers looks slowly around.
Off in the distance they spy the bright light
and march towards it knowing it is right.

Soon they can see a shining white tower
that dazzles and shimmers with awesome power.
A voice from within is heard sharp as ice.
"You better stop there and tell me you are nice."

Remembering the rhyme, they call out in alarm,
that they are friendly travellers and mean no harm.
"I am the diamond fairy and I will let you pass."
Says a much kinder voice without any fuss.

On entering the hall through a tall sparkling door,
they can see a glass throne that sits on the floor.
A beautiful white fairy all covered in fine lace,
sits up quite straight and looks them square in the face.

As quick as can be, they relate their sad tale
and ask the diamond fairy if she can help them prevail.
She looks down with a frown and after some reflection,
looks up again, and smiles in their direction.

"I believe my three sisters may help in your quest,
but I only know where one of them currently rests.
The ruby fairy sits in a tall tree,
surrounded in mist, so no one can see."

Without further discussion, they all rise and depart
with the diamond fairy, who joins them in good heart.
In a few moments, the dragons are in the air,
the wind rushing at speed through everyone's hair.

The diamond fairy sits in the front,
giving directions to all in the hunt.
Over the mountains they approach a great mist,
but they cannot go-round, as the way may be missed.

The cloud is so great that it is hard to see,
and within a few minutes they bump into a tree.
With cries of alarm they fall off their steeds,
but land on soft grass, so nobody bleeds.

From high in the branches, a voice can be heard,
the sound of which is just like a sweet bird.
"I am the ruby fairy. Who is knocking on my door?
I can see you all clearly, sitting on the floor."

The diamond fairy calls out very fast,
and tells the tale, so no spells will be cast.
The ruby fairy now understands
and tells them of the emerald fairy's lands.

"It is full of evil goblins and elves," she cries.
"You will have to be brave and fight for your lives."
Shields and swords appear at the click of her fingers,
while they dress in bright armour, nobody lingers.

They mount their dragons which are eager to run,
and the ruby fairy shouts that she must also come.
Princess Phoenix makes room by her side,
and is joined by her new friend, who comes for the ride.

In a moment they rise up in the sky,
flying over mountains that seem very high.
Through rain and snow, the team advances,
each looking to the other with nervous glances.

After a while the warm sun comes out,
and princess Belinda alerts them with a shout.
Below there is a valley that is lush and green,
it is a place where no one has been.

The squadron flies low and breaks formation,
each looking to find the emerald fairy's nation.
A meadow by a river seems the right place,
but prince Ryan has a frown on his face.

As the dragons settle gently in the tall grass,
small figures leap from shadows in the pass.
Attacked by goblins armed with short swords,
they lift their shields, against the massed hordes.

The air is filled with yells and wild shouts,
with heads and shoulders receiving big clouts.
The noise is tremendous, and no one can think,
it is not helped at all by the goblins' stink.

Backwards and forwards the battle rages,
the travellers seem to fight for ages.
Each princess is valiant and true,
nobody can win against this bold crew.

Swords and shields clash with great sparks,
each becomes dented, with plenty of marks.
Puffing and panting, they carry on fighting.
Up in the sky there is thunder and lightning.

Awoken by the great noise, the dragons are alert,
and do not want to see their friends getting hurt.
All as one, they rise in the sky,
each one making a most terrible cry.

Swooping down, from a great height,
the dragons prepare to join the fight.
They open their mouths, which start to glow,
and out shoot hot flames that reach down below.

Within a few minutes, the battle is no more,
the goblins have disappeared from the floor.
Nothing is left to show they were there,
not even a wisp of their curly black hair

The circle of friends stands and give a cheer,
as each of the dragons land quite near.
With laughter and smiles, they review their position,
and are pleased to see they are in good condition.

The two fairies appear and approach at a run,
to remind the victors there is still work to be done.
"The emerald fairy has to be found without any rest
if you want to complete all of this quest."

Princess Angeli uses her skill
and swiftly runs to the top of the hill.
Looking carefully with all of her power,
she sees a green castle that has a tall tower.

Without hesitation, they mount most swiftly,
and fly off towards the hidden city.
The light becomes pale, and music sounds sprightly,
as they land on the castle, ever so lightly.

A voice within asks them to walk through the door,
where they see small figures grouped on the floor.
All dressed in bright green it is a beautiful scene,
but they are looking for the emerald queen.

As if she knows that it is time to appear,
the emerald fairy lets them know she is here
"I hear you have beaten the goblin king
and you have flown very far, upon a large wing."

Smiling and graceful, the emerald fairy calls a hush,
as her two sisters explain their quest in a rush.
Not to be left out, the princesses all shout,
to help reveal what all the fuss is about.

After the tale has been told in a great hurry,
the group of travellers sit down in a flurry.
Exhausted and tired after the day's wild events,
they move on to rest in some lovely warm tents.

The three princesses are first to nod off,
soon from the others, there is not even a cough.
The emerald fairy pretends to sleep,
but a secret meeting she will keep.

Dressed in her long flowing robe,
she reaches out for her magic globe.
As the mist clears away, she sees with alarm
a grey-bearded wizard, but he can do no harm.

"Where is the blue fairy?" She nicely asks,
hoping that the wizard will help with the tasks.
With a look of concern, he reaches out his arm
and looks down at the globe that sits in his palm.

"She's been taken by trolls' and thrown down a well,
I do not know where, but your elf friends may tell."
The wizard looks up, and the connection is broken,
and the emerald fairy looks for her elf token.

She searches in drawers without making a peep,
not to disturb her guests, who are fast asleep.
At last, the elf token is found in a tub,
and the emerald fairy gives it a good rub.

In a flash and a bang, the elf king appears.
The noise has awoken her guests, she fears.
Her worst suspicion is confirmed in her ear,
as a voice from behind speaks loud and clear.

Princess Indigo, who shows no fear,
asks. "Who is that, and why is he here?"
"None of your business," is the reply,
hoping that the response will not make her cry.

"That's rather rude actually", the princess retorts,
and spins on her heels to make her reports.
The others wake and demand to be updated,
as the emerald fairy is about to be berated.

The elf king speaks loudly in her defence,
confirming to all that she meant no offence.
Calm and collected, the emerald fairy recovers
and asks if the trolls' well is known to the others.

They all sit down and work out the plan
to search for the blue fairy as quick as they can.
After a moment, the elf king agrees
to guide them through the very tall trees.

Up in the air, they all look so scary,
including the elf king and the emerald fairy.
The dragons fly higher, far to the north,
until they can see tall trees coming forth.

Looking down as best they are able,
princess Phoenix spies the troll's table.
The dragons circle and prepare to land,
ready to release their warrior band.

As they approach the trolls' scruffy camp,
the fairies gather and light a bright lamp.
In the strong light, the trolls start to moan.
Gradually they freeze and turn to stone.

Now that the trolls' powers have vanished,
they all look for the well before it is banished
In only a few minutes, they hear a faint cry,
and lo and behold, the well is found dry.

There is no mistake, a blue light can be seen,
coming from the well in a bright shining beam.
A rope is lowered,,and much to their delight,
the blue fairy leaps out and into the light.

Refreshed and revived, the blue fairy looks around.
She is delighted to be back on safe ground.
With kisses and hugs they greet the missing sister
telling her how they had really missed her.

Now the fairy sisters are together,
they discuss the witch's spell and the bad weather.
The blue fairy looks in her old book of magic
to find a solution for something so tragic.

Looking up at last from her reading,
the blue fairy's face is seen to be beaming.
"I have the solution to this evil deed,
we must return to the castle at high speed."

With a loud cheer and a roar of delight,
the travellers set off on their flight.
Over the forests, they travel very fast.
Nobody wants to arrive late or be the last.

It seems that with their magic powers,
the castle appears, with its tall towers.
The ground is wet and covered with puddles,
it can be seen that everyone struggles.

Without a moment to lose, they land in the rain,
stepping carefully over a flooded deep drain.
As the castle door is thrown wide open,
the blue fairy brings out the magic token.

King Mark laughs with sheer delight,
but naturally, they all look a terrible sight.
Queen Olivia greets them with smiles of contentment
and insists that they partake of some refreshment.

Telling their story without missing a beat,
they sit down and have plenty to eat.
The blue fairy, however, is not happy at all,
and insists they move to the great hall.

"We, the four fairy sisters, must gather around
and let the three princesses sit on the ground.
As soon as the magic circle is completed,
the evil spell can be defeated."

Without delay, the blue fairy shows them the token
and tells them how the magic words can be spoken.
As the words fall gently from their lips,
the rain gradually turns to just a few drips.

In a few moments, the sun shines in the sky,
and all the puddles begin to dry.
Everyone gets excited and runs in the warm air,
nobody is downhearted or gives a care.

The three princesses turn to the fairies four,
and thank them all for settling the score.
It was the blue fairy, they say together.
She was the one who corrected the weather.

"Yes," say the princesses, in their own way.
"It was the blue fairy who saved the day".
"What of the evil witch?" I hear you say.
Well, that is a story for another day!

The End

This book would not have been possible without the support and encouragement of my wife, Helen, and of course my three grandchildren, Angeli, Indigo and Phoenix, who were instrumental in the creation of the story, together with the rest of my family, who each had a part to play.

I would also like to thank my good friend, and fellow author, Clive La Pensee, for his help in editing and proof reading.

There must also be a very special thank you to Maddie Egremont, who has brought the story to life with her beautiful illustrations.

2nd Edition - Published in 2021 by:

WALLBOOKS
22, Queensmead Avenue
Epsom, Surrey. KT17 3EQ
www.mswallbooks.com

All enquiries should be addressed to: WALLBOOKS
Cover design by Maddie Egremont
ISBN: 979-8-716674-14-1
Printed in the U.K

Printed in Great Britain
by Amazon